GIVING HONOR TO MY PASTOR

A Tribute to
Dr. Joseph Arnold King

Volume 1

BY NORMAN H. LYONS, JR.

GIVING HONOR TO MY PASTOR

A Tribute to
Dr. Joseph Arnold King

Volume 1

BY NORMAN H. LYONS, JR.

NUVISION PUBLISHING

Books may be ordered through booksellers
or by contacting:

Norman H. Lyons, Jr.
P.O. Box 86
Uniondale NY 11553

ISBN# 978-1-5136-8319-5

PO Box 4455 | Wilmington NC
www.nuvisiondesigns.biz

Printed in the United States of America.

DEDICATION

It is with great honor and appreciation that I dedicate this book in loving memory of Mother Mabel King and Supt. Arcell Vickers Sr.

TABLE OF CONTENTS

ACKNOWLEDGEMENTS

This book would not be possible without the historical perspective of Elder Walter Davis (Dr. King's grandson) who shared with me so much information. Dr. King would be so proud of your ability to retain and recall pertinent facts about him and the history of the churches that he served.

God Bless Mother Betty Jean Davis (the daughter of Dr. King) who is the sweet songbird of our era. Thank you for sharing your parents with us.

Likewise, I would not have been able to complete this project without the intense interviews with Supt. Arcell Vickers, Sr., State Supervisor Marion Vickers, National Evangelist Sheila Vickers, and the love and support of the entire Vickers Family.

I greatly appreciate all of the advice and administrative ability of Shelley Brazley who has preserved the J A King Project.

To my theological brother Rev. Kirk D. Lyons, Sr. I must say, "It was you who cracked the case and solved the mystery of the obituary." Thanks for your keen observation.

To my precious wife, Sharon Elaine, who constantly supports all of my endeavors, thank you for your love and commitment. To my daughters Juliet and Jasmine, who are my inspirations to write for future generations. To my son-in-law, Joaquin, Juliet's husband, who constantly looks out for his new "Dad."

Thank God for The Fountain of Life Church who affords me the respect and freedom to be who God called me to be. You are a stupendous blessing.

Finally, I must acknowledge my mother, Mother Gladys Virginia Lyons, for her adamant adherence to saving church programs of historic events. Because of her, I had an original copy of the Homegoing Service for Dr. King.

Giving Honor to My Pastor
A Tribute to Dr. Joseph Arnold King

INTRODUCTION

One night I had a dream that I had gone to heaven. Upon my arrival I was greeted by Mother Reba Cummings. Mother Cummings is the first-born daughter of Dr. Joseph and Mother Mable King. She was obviously in a glorified state. Her skin was glowing. Her smile was sparkling, and her movements were fluid. Yet, her hair was still in a bun (smile). After she welcomed me, she began to thank me over and over again. As I was wondering why, I suddenly woke up.

As I sought the Lord for an interpretation of the dream, He revealed to me the meaning. He explained that Mother Cummings was thanking me for completing the assignment of writing a book about her father. Her father was Dr. Joseph Arnold King. He was the Pastor of King's Temple Church Of God In Christ (COGIC) in Hempstead, NY and the founder and Pastor of King's Chapel COGIC in Southampton, NY. Although I tremble at the task of such a daunting assignment, it is an undeserved privilege to be called to compose a tribute to one of my Pastors.

Dr. King was the most beloved Pastor I have ever known. His flock loved loving him and giving him honor. Two of the young people who were members of Kings Temple attended my elementary school. They were constantly speaking well of their Pastor and First Lady. Their high esteem for their leaders inspired me to visit their church. It was there that I met the man God would use to transform my life.

In 2010, God inspired Shelley Brazley (One of Dr. King's daughters in the faith) to organize a weekend celebration for "The Saints of Our Youth." On that occasion we honored our spiritual fathers and mothers from Kings Temple and Kings Chapel. We were amazed to see that so many of our senior saints were alive and strong. This was a testament to our beloved Pastor King. Not only was he fruitful but his fruit yet remained. Dr. King went home to be with the Lord on August 25, 1978. Thirty-two years later, the seniors, spiritual sons, and daughters came from all over the country to honor our living elders in the faith. In that one setting we saw the multi-generational impact of our Pastor. We counted four generations of believers represented that weekend.

A preliminary fund raiser was hosted by Mason Temple COGIC and Superintendent Arcell Vickers (Dr. King's Armor Bearer). The rehearsal for the concert was hosted by Kings Temple and Bishop Milton Rochford (Dr. King's successor). The banquet for the senior saints was hosted by Fountain of Life Church and Yours Truly. The concert was hosted by Perfecting Faith Church and Pastor Donnie McClurkin. One successor and three spiritual sons hosted this colossal event while an executive committee comprised of spiritual sons and daughters coordinated the event. When I looked out over the sea of people that Dr. King had served, I thought to myself, Dr. King was greater than we thought he was. He was greater than we thought because his fruit remained and his spiritual seed is mighty upon the earth. Therefore, the time has come for Dr. King to be acknowledged and honored in a tributary document.

Originally, I intended to conduct extensive interviews with people that Dr. King served. In fact, I did have a few intense interviews for which I am grateful. There are so many people who knew Dr. King longer and more personally than I did. That's why I was so comfortable depending on their accounts to formulate my manuscript. Unfortunately, my plans were not fulfilled, and time restraints would not permit me to wait any longer. Nevertheless, it is my endeavor to document my personal experience with Dr. King, in the hope of compiling tributes from a host of others in the future.

Allow me to be perfectly clear from the start. This book is a testimonial tribute to one of my Pastors. It is my intention to sanctify my leader in the eyes of the people. One of my mentors taught me: *"Never criticize a man you can't outproduce."* Although I have heard less than flattering comments and even criticisms about Dr. King, his works far outweigh those words. Few men in the ministry in our region have outproduced my beloved Pastor. It is not just what he did, but it was when he did it that makes him so great.

Chapter One

Where Is the Obituary?

As I was conducting interviews and gathering information, I was asking everyone I could think of for a copy of Dr. King's homegoing program. I wanted to read the obituary. Much to my chagrin, I was disappointed that nobody seemed to have an obituary from Dr. King's homecoming service. Expressing my dismay to my brother, Reverend Kirk Lyons, Sr., he said, "Man… if anybody has a copy of that obituary it would be Mommy. And if she has it, it would be in her huge family Bible." I said to him, "That Bible is packed away in a box in my garage." He said to me, "The answer might very well be in your own house." On Wednesday night, February 17th, 2021, I found out my brother was right.

As I was cleaning up my garage in preparation for the impending snowstorm, I opened the box where my mother's huge family Bible was stored. As I looked through the Bible, I noticed a whole host of official documents especially funeral programs. Much to my surprise, as I flipped through the pages, I happened upon the program for Dr. Joseph Arnold King's homegoing. I screamed so loud that my wife called me on my cell phone to make sure I was alright. I explained to her I had just found the program I had been asking others about for over a year. I called my brother to tell him he was right. The answer was in my own house for nine years and I didn't even know it. This was truly a sign from God to move forward with the process.

-------The Life of Dr. Joseph Arnold King-------

According to the obituary, Dr. King was born on March 28, 1900 in Walter Hill, TN. He was the second child of Jimmy and Betty King. At a very young age, Dr. King moved to St. Louis and matriculated through the Elementary and High School system. He considered St. Louis his home. Dr. King professed his faith in Jesus Christ at a very young age and decided to dedicate his life to preaching the gospel. As a young man Dr. King was an evangelist who traveled across the country. He earned a reputation as one of the most outstanding evangelists with miracles and signs following his ministry. In one of my interviews, it was stated that as a young woman, Mother Mabel Andrews was an anointed singer. It was also mentioned that as she sang the sermonic solo before Evangelist Joseph King preached, he fell in love with her, and knew she was his wife. However, Dr. King shared with me a slightly different take on his attraction to Mother Mabel King. One Sunday afternoon while I was serving as his bodyguard, he told me the following story. He said that after one of his evangelistic services a young woman by the name of Mabel was assigned the task of serving him his dinner. He said she also served him some sweet potatoe pie that she had made. He said when he tasted that pie, he knew she was his wife and decided he was going to marry her. He shook his head and said, "It was that pie." Suffice it to say, it probably was her singing, her cooking, and the will of God. He married the love of his life, Mabel Andrews on August 29th, 1923.

From this union two lovely daughters were born, Mrs. Reba Jo King Cummings and Mrs. Betty Jean King Davis. The obituary reveals some pertinent facts about Dr. King's previous pastorates before he came to New York. Dr. King's first pastorate was in Pratt City, Alabama, where there is a church dedicated in his memory. His second pastoral assignment was in Lancaster, PA. Then Dr. King came to Hempstead, NY in 1929 and "settled at King's Temple COGIC" which would be his third pastoral assignment. Dr. King also founded and shepherded King's Chapel in Southampton, NY. This means that Dr. King pastored four churches in his lifetime and erected two church buildings that are standing to this day.

In addition to all of his pastoral labor, Dr. King continued his theological studies. I have read biographical accounts that indicated he became a Hebrew scholar and earned his Doctor of Divinity degree from Columbia University.

One day I noticed that Dr. King had absolutely no clutter in his office. However, there were pictures of astute looking gray haired caucasian gentlemen on the wall. When I asked Brother Arcell Vickers, Sr. about it, he told me that those men were Dr. King's professors. There is a paragraph in the obituary that states, in addition to his earned degrees: *"Dr. King has received many awards and honorary degrees from individuals and institutions who recognized and acknowledged his brilliant contributions in the field of religion."*

When Dr. King's health began to fail, he desired to return back to St. Louis to be with his brother, Richard King and his sister, Mrs. Ida McDow. His daughter Mrs. Reba Cummings, Brother and Sister Vickers, and Brother Willard Meeks, Sr. accompanied him back home. After arriving in St. Louis, on August 20th, 1978 he entered St. Mary's Hospital. It was there that he made his transition from earth to glory at 4:05 pm on August 25th, 1978.

It is utterly amazing how God weaves our lives together for His purpose. With all that Dr. King was doing when I walked through the vestibule of Kings' Temple for the first time, he found time to impact my life forever.

21

Chapter Two

The Sunday Morning Entrance

While sitting in the pew of Kings' Temple waiting for the service to begin for the first time, nobody prepared me for what was about to happen. I had seen processionals. I had experienced being ordered to stand when the Bishop entered the church or pulpit. But nowhere had I seen an entrance of a pastor like Dr. Joseph Arnold King. The doors were opened by an usher and then this stately gray-haired man dressed similar to a priest would appear and walk down the center aisle. As he was walking, the people in the church would reach out and touch him as he made his way to the pulpit.

There have been some who have made derogatory statements about this routine entrance. However, the Bible says, judge nothing before the time. Although I was shocked the first time I saw it, I was intrigued by it and asked my classmates to explain it. They informed me that people had been healed by touching Dr. King's garments, his arms and hands. I could relate to that because I grew up in a "signs and wonders" church. More importantly, there was Bible to back it up *(Matthew 9:20-22)*. Yet rarely did you find a local pastor who walked in that anointing on a regular basis.

Eventually, I got used to "the entrance" especially since it happened every Sunday morning that he was at the Hempstead church. Although it took me some time, eventually I began to reach out and touch the man of God. In fact, I don't ever remember being sick the whole time I was a member of Kings' Temple. Dr. King wasn't just walking down the aisle, he was walking in the power and demonstration of the Holy Spirit.

Men and women with a prophetic mantle on their life are quite different and distinct from everybody else. They are peculiar and particular in the execution of their ministry. Their ears are pressing ever close to the mouth of God. Their eyes are looking beyond yonder to see what others cannot see. They also pay a high price for their intimate walk with God. Those of us that are blessed to have them as shepherds are the beneficiaries of their sufferings. Therefore, you should never mock a person for how God decides to use them. I'd rather have a pastor who walks down the center aisle in the power and demonstration of the Holy Ghost, than a pastor who walks in darkness and has no power over sickness and disease. I'd rather have a pastor who is an over-comer rather than a pastor who is being overcome.

A testimony beats an argument any day.

A work of manifestation beats a word of mockery any day. Allow me to admit, of course, I am defensive of my pastor. Especially, when he is being mischaracterized and mocked publicly. At some point it is incumbent upon someone that took the time to get an understanding, to explain the entrance phenomenon properly. Although I will never forget the shock of seeing it for the first time, I am also glad I kept coming back to the church. It afforded me the privilege to eventually serve an anointed and astute man of God.

Dr. King was the most unique and inimitable man I have ever known. He did a whole lot during a time when our people were working with very little. Dr. King used public transportation to get to church for quite a long time. He walked, rode buses, and took trains to get to both churches until the saints took responsibility to drive him. So yes, God allowed him to walk on water a little bit on Sunday mornings. We, the people, of his flock had no problem with it.

Chapter Three

A Slap Tap on the Face

The King's Temple Choir was one of the premier gospel choirs of the seventies. The story behind this legendary choir deserves to be written in its own book. Nevertheless, no matter where we travelled on the weekend, we had to be in the choir loft on Sunday mornings for morning worship.

The pulpit of King's Temple was situated between the north and south sides of the choir loft at that time. It was a most unique architectural arrangement that positioned Dr. King in the middle with choristers on each side of him. As Dr. King entered his golden years, the church purchased a special swivel pulpit chair for him. This allowed him to save his legs and spin around as he ministered.

Dr. King had a peculiar technique of getting his point across to individuals directly during his Sunday morning message. Whenever he wanted to make a personal point to someone, he would call them up to stand next to him in the pulpit. Then he would turn in his chair, look them straight in the eye, and give them what I call a "slap tap on the face."

A few Sundays he would call me up by saying, "Tall Boy." That was his first nickname for me. He never got used to calling me by my proper name. But he had nicknames for a lot of his members. When he called me, I stood up and went up to the pulpit and stood beside him. He turned in his swivel chair and looked me straight in my eyes and slapped tapped me on the face. Then, I just turned around and took my seat in the choir stand. I came to understand the significance of this peculiar gesture. For the older preachers in Pentecost this was a form of rebuke. I remember seeing it as a boy growing up around a lot of the Pentecostal pioneers in the area. Being honest about it, each time Dr. King gave me a "slap tap" I understood exactly why he did it. I was just relieved that he didn't tell the whole church why he did it. He didn't miss it not one time. One Sunday he called me up and I said to myself, "Oh my God, what did I do now?" To my surprise Dr. King told the story about how a drunk man on the elevator of his apartment building made a sudden move towards him and how I reacted. This was the first time Brother Vickers allowed me to escort Dr. King to his apartment alone. Which meant Dr. King was solely in my care. I followed the example and instructions of Brother Vickers to the letter.

As we were on the elevator, this drunken man started using profanity and made a sudden move towards Dr. King. I reacted quickly to pin him against the wall with one arm and guided Dr. King safely off the elevator with my other arm. It all happened so quickly that the man and Dr. King were startled. Dr. King took a deep sigh of relief and the man was relieved that I let him go. After a strong threat, I did let him go.

Dr. King waited about two months before he said anything about that night. Yet on this particular Sunday, Dr. King recounted that night and called me his "Champion." From that Sunday forth, he called me "Champion." I thought I was going to get another "slap tap" but I received a new name.

Chapter Four

Finding the Treasure In the Temple

One Saturday, I observed that Brother Johnnie was cleaning the church all by himself. I said to myself, "This church is too big for one man to clean all by himself." So, I took it upon myself to volunteer to help him. At first, he said, "That's OK. I can do it." But I kept asking and he eventually tested me out on some small tasks. Then he gave me larger tasks until one Saturday he let me clean the entire upstairs.

I would clean the sanctuary first, then the ladies lounge (which was Mother Mabel King's office when she was alive). Then I would clean Dr. King's office which was on the opposite side of the hallway.

One Saturday while cleaning the ladies lounge, I noticed a stack of magazines in a rack. When I picked up one of the magazines, I realized it was a journal from a Holy Convocation convened in Memphis Tennessee. As I read through this journal, I realized that it had pictures, articles and historical information about this annual meeting. The next time I cleaned the top floor of the church I read the next journal.

Each week after cleaning the church I would read another journal until eventually I read all the journals that went so far back in history that they had pictures of people riding horses to get to the convocation.

I systemically read every journal from beginning to end. Then I would start from the top of the stack to the bottom all over again. This is one of the ways I educated myself about the Church Of God In Christ. My ritual was to clean the church and then lay down on the floor of the ladies' lounge, read, and pray. I would pray about what I read and ask God to use me like he did the men and women of God in that era.

Although I never met Mother Mabel King, she is

responsible for helping me learn about the history of our beloved denomination. Because she saved those journals and kept them in pristine condition, I was able to read about the formative years of the church. The best part of cleaning the church was finding the treasure of history in the ladies' lounge.

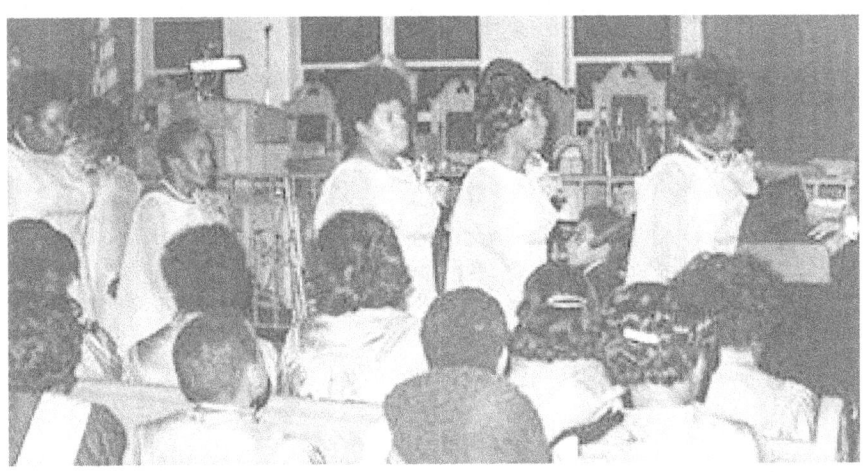

37

41

Mother
Betty Jean Davis

Chapter Five

Down in the Basement

There was a precious saint in King's Temple named Mother Pearl Williams. Besides being a prayer warrior, one of her jobs was to clean the basement bathrooms and floors. She drafted me to help her because she said she couldn't get down on the hard floor anymore because of her weakened knees. So, she trained me to do it. Little did I know what I had gotten myself into. The first thing she taught me was that I couldn't stand up and do the job right. I had to get down on my knees in order to scrub the floors correctly. She filled the bucket with all the cleaning liquids and Ajax. Then she gave me the brush and explained how to dip the brush into the bucket and spread the detergent onto the floor and scrub.

I couldn't believe that I was actually, on my hands and knees scrubbing floors.

Mother Williams would guide me over every inch of the basement floor. She was standing and walking while I was kneeling and scrubbing. All the while she was preaching to me. She would tell me I could make it in life no matter what the devil said or did. Then she would tell me how much God was going to bless me for working in the church. She would always tell her testimony about how God kept her strong and supplied all her needs. She made it clear to me that Dr. King had high standards for the cleanliness of the church. She always said, "This church has to be clean." She would say, "When I'm dead and gone and if you're here you make sure this church is clean." Then she would talk very plainly about how she felt about how some people mistreated and neglected God's house.

The thing that stuck with me the most, however, was her awareness of how high of a standard Dr. King set for the cleanliness of the church. Mother Williams accepted her assignment seriously and made sure those floors were cleaned up to Dr. King's specifications. When the job was done, she would pull out this little purse full of cash and offer me some money for working. I told her, "Mother I can't accept that." She would try to convince me, but I told her my mother would not approve of me accepting money from her. She said, "Well I don't won't you to get in trouble with your mother, so let me pray for you."

Trust me her prayers were more valuable than her money.

She prayed some prayers for me down in the basement that blessed me in the pulpit. I learned a lot about Dr. King from the older saints in the church that he and Mother King personally taught and trained. They were the standard bearers of the church and they never ceased to tell you what Dr. King taught them.

Chapter Six
From Singing to Serving

One Sunday morning as I was sitting in the choir stand, Brother Vickers came and told me that Dr. King wanted me to come and sit next to him. Dr. King had a habit of sitting on the back pew against the wall on hot and humid Sundays. So, without hesitation I quickly got up and followed Brother Vickers to the back of the church. He told me where to sit and placed this huge wicker fan in my hand and told me to fan Dr. King slowly. Of course, I did it just as I was instructed not realizing that this simple act marked the beginning of the end of my singing ministry in Kings Temple. Meaning, singing would never be number one again. Serving Dr. King under the supervision of Brother Vickers would be my primary obligation.

The next Sunday, Brother Vickers did the same thing, he came up to the choir stand and asked me to sit next to Dr. King and fan him. Eventually after singing I would just walk to the back of the church and wait for Dr. King to come in and fan him. Little did I know that there were graduating levels of responsibility involved with serving Dr. King. Each assignment, done correctly, would lead to another. My next assignment was to sit with him after the service while he ate his dinner. My responsibility was to fan the flies away and protect him from anyone who would disturb him. This allowed Brother Vickers time to eat with his family and come back for the next shift which involved driving Dr. King all the way to Kings Chapel in Southampton.

Dr. King was a man of very few words. He would sit and eat and be absolutely silent, but one day he shocked me by breaking the silence. He said, "I knew your father…" I was blown away. I didn't think he knew anything about my family background. Growing up in Hempstead, I should have known better. The second time Dr. King spoke to me after he ate his meal, he said something that I didn't repeat to anybody until after I had been in ministry for quite a while. He closed his eyes and leaned backwards and said, "You have a divine calling on your life." Then he opened his eyes and leaned forward as though he didn't say anything at all. His words were few but powerful and profitable.

The first time I was asked to accompany Dr. King to the evening service in Southampton was the beginning of yet another level of responsibility. Brother Vickers explained that when you ride with Dr. King you have to be quiet and not speak at all unless he asks you a question. This was the rule, if he was silent you must be silent. There was no way I could have known how long the ride to Southampton was. As the ride got longer and longer, I thought "Where in the world are we going?"

When we finally arrived, I proceeded to remove Dr. King's luggage and we walked into this well-built Chapel like church. It was just as clean and neat as Kings Temple. The people were gracious and attentive to Dr. King just like the saints in Hempstead. It was a Sunday night service and I then realized the grueling schedule Dr. King and Brother Vickers maintained. If Dr. King was at the

Hempstead church on Sunday morning, he was at the Southampton church on Sunday evening. The next week he would reverse the order.

In those days I had a well-earned reputation for being outspoken, but I could be quiet. In Dr. King's presence you had to be quiet because he was a man of solitude and meditation. I truly thank God for Brother Vickers who would eventually become a pastor, superintendent, and an administrative assistant to a jurisdictional bishop. He was the one that taught and trained me to serve a leader. He explained that I had to adjust to the demeanor of the leader. He let me know what an honor it was to be allowed to serve the pastor.

One of my bishops said to me, "My most loyal and faithful sons have come from the Church Of God In Christ." He said, "What do they do to you in that church?" We laughed and then I said, "As for me it was a man by the name of Brother Arcell Vickers. He trained me to serve my leader." He said, "I hope one day I get to meet him to tell him what a great job he did with you."

Serving Dr. King was really assisting Brother Vickers who served the pastor. I received my orders from him. Brother Vickers gave the orders and I carried them out to the best of my ability. This experience was a major turning point in my life. It afforded me the privilege to be in the presence of a real prophet of God. I didn't know how this assignment would be a perpetual blessing in my life. God bless the day Brother Vickers called me out of the choir loft.

One Saturday, Brother Vickers contacted me and said, "Today we are going to paint the church steeple." We went to the store and purchased the supplies and returned to the church. Brother Vickers set up the ladder and instructed me to climb up to the steeple. I had a fear of heights and was petrified. Up to that point, I had never disobeyed a direct order from Brother Vickers. Because I didn't want to let him down and knowing how important the physical appearance of the church was to Dr. King, I was compelled to overcome my fear. I explained to Brother Vickers that I had never been up this high before and I needed him to tell me exactly what to do. Long story short, he did, I did, and the job got done.

That Sunday he gave Dr. King a full report and proudly told him to look up at the steeple. The look on Dr. King's face paid for it all. He looked so pleased and proud and that was a priceless pay off for me.

One hot Sunday afternoon, Brother Vickers told me Dr. King wanted some ice cream from Carvel. Little did I know this was a major deal. The Carvel Shop was off of Peninsula Blvd. and our church was on Laurel Ave., a considerable distance away. My task was to purchase the ice cream cone and walk it back to the church before it melted. This meant that I had to walk fast, but I had to maintain my balance, or else the cone would fall. I figured out it would be best if I walked under the shade of the trees along the way as much as I could. When I walked in the sun, I covered the cone with my hand, creating a small shade. I say this to say: any assignment you were given in King's Temple that related to Dr. King was a big deal. It had to be done a certain way in a specific time frame. Dr. King had high standards and I excelled in environments such as that. I enjoyed the challenge. Dr. King's standard influenced me for the rest of my life in that I was able to serve bishops from all types of denominations around the country and in various parts of the world.

Although there are other substantial chores I performed around the church, I am convinced that what I have written is sufficient to describe the servitude experience afforded me by Dr. King and Brother Arcell Vickers. It was a **HIGH HONOR** to be called upon to serve at such a young age and I shall never take it lightly. Allow me to summarize this season with an old quotation that states:

"Any job big or small, do it right, or not at all."

Chapter Seven

Can We Go Bowling?

When we were teenagers growing up in the church, two of the major issues were going bowling and to the movies. As simple as it may sound today, back then it was a controversial issue. Being that I was trained to respect the older saints in the church, I was not going to argue with them about it. In fact, until I reached a certain age, I didn't even want to go to the movies. Church was the best show in town for real. We had live music, singing, preaching, and if the truth be told, a whole lot of acting too.

When I landed at King's Temple there was a small army of young people. Trust me. We had fun. We enjoyed the older saints because they were so animated you couldn't help but love them. We enjoyed each other because we had a lot in common growing up in a "sanctified" church. However, we had a dilemma. We were being told that in our church bowling was forbidden. I heard a lot of older saints say it, but I never remembered hearing Dr. King say anything about it. So, I had the bright idea of just simply going to the Pastor and asking him. I followed the protocol by telling Brother Vickers I had a question for Dr. King. I told him what the question was, and he said be patient and I will speak to the Pastor about it. I thanked him and quite frankly I forgot about it.

One night while we were taking Dr. King home, Brother Vickers caught me off guard and said, "Dr. King, Brother Lyons has a question he would like to ask you." I was nervous. I didn't quite know what to expect but I knew a lot was riding on how I asked this question. I said, "Dr. King, I just wanted to know if the young people could go bowling." I said, "I will do whatever you say. I just want to know what the rule is."

Dr. King waited for a while. He looked out the window, took his time and softly said, "I would rather you go together. You can go, if you go together." When I told the young people what Dr. King said, it was cause for great joy.

Oh, how I wish the story ended there but it doesn't. I had to take a beating in the court of public opinion because some powerful people didn't believe Dr. King gave us his consent. I understood it and accepted that this was a generational divide. Yet I was so proud of my Pastor who transcended the norms of the former days and kept his young people connected to the church.

His genius was expressed in that he didn't just release us to go bowling in general. He wisely attached a stipulation to it "Go together." That is exactly what we did. The fall out was not his fault. It was just a generational situation. He answered my question with wisdom and understanding. It was a great lesson in pastoral leadership.

Chapter Eight

College is Calling

One of the greatest transitions in life is going from high school to college. My high school years were very dynamic and unique because of the huge success of our local church choir. The King's Temple Choir was the most innovative and provocative choir of the seventies. There was another choir that was historically more productive than we were. However, we created a new sound that spawned and inspired many of the gospel artists of this day.

What many people don't know was that the roots of the choir's success can be traced back to the musicality of our pastor, Dr. King.

When Dr. King told me the story of how he met Mother Mabel King, he also shared with me that he attended Oberlin College and studied music. It was reported to me that he also played for Bishop C. H. Mason on some occasions. In some of my interviews, it was expressed to me that in his younger days, Dr. King played all the instruments, and taught the church classical hymns.

As he got older, he prayed that God would impart his gifts to his children and the saints. And that's what happened. By the time I arrived at King's Temple, I had never been in a church where so many people could play the organ and piano.

His grandson, *the legendary Professor Benny Cummings,* was an extra ordinary choir master and director. He was an exceptional arranger and a supreme stage performer. Elder Cummings was far ahead of his time and our talented musicians could embellish and transform his renditions into masterpieces.

The choir was composed of seasoned saints and talented young people. We prayed incessantly before a note was sung in rehearsal. Rehearsals were brutal and eternal, but the combination of prayer and practice made us ballistic in church and on stage. We were in demand and it was a most exciting time for us.

As time progressed, the high school students had to start preparing for college. As much as I loved singing with the choir, I wanted to go away to attend school. When I got accepted to Syracuse University, there was a contingent of people that didn't think I would leave. Mother Reba Cummings asked my mother when I was born. When my mother told her, Mother Cummings told everybody, "Leave him alone. He's going. He made up his mind and he's going."

The next thing on my agenda was to locate a Church of God in Christ in Syracuse. I informed Dr. King that I had been accepted to the University and I wanted to be referred to a church within our denomination in the area. He said he would get back to me. On the last Sunday before I had to leave, I was summoned into his office and he wrote on a piece of paper: "Payton's Temple COGIC." As destiny would have it, this was the church where I met my wife of over 41 years at the time of this writing. Little did I know that the note he wrote would be the last instruction he would directly give me. I am so glad I followed through and obeyed him. Because it was in Payton's Temple that I preached my trial sermon on the last Sunday night in January 1979.

Epilogue

Throughout my time at King's Temple, the older saints would talk about what a phenomenal preacher Dr. King was. During my time there, he focused on teaching and prophesying. I never heard him "whoop" in the tradition of the black church, except for one night at a District meeting in Queens, NY. The church accompanied him. The choir sang. The District conducted their business and then Dr. King was introduced to bring forth the word.

Dr. King was dressed meticulously as usual. He always presented himself as a quintessential well-dressed gentleman. He proceeded to honor the house, took his text, and after about 15 minutes it happened. Being that I was in the choir and his servant, I had a good seat close behind him and I could see what was about to happen from a vantage point.

My Pastor, Dr. Joseph Arnold King, lifted up his voice and held his note in perfect key. When he did that, it was like a mighty wind rushed through that church. I looked at the windows to see if they were opened but they were closed. It was the wind of the anointing that kept on blowing. Dr. King kept building and climbing in his velocity and it was like the earth shook under my feet. I tell you, it felt like the earth moved. In all my days growing up in the church, I never saw or felt something like that.

The intensity reached a point where he knew the congregation couldn't take any more and he promptly took his seat. The church went into pandemonium. It was in that moment I understood the older saint's fascination, endearment, and solidarity to Dr. King. They remembered what it was like to be under a young Dr. King. That night I got a glimpse of it and it was cataclysmic.

In that one service, I was given a snapshot of the evangelistic anointing upon my pastor. He never lost it, but he accepted the assignment and the season of life he was in.

Dr. King was a man of prayer. Dr. King was a true prophet. Dr. King was a builder. Dr. King was a scholar. Dr. King was a man, husband, and father. As a spiritual father, I was always safe in his presence. He never spoke out of turn. He never asked me to do anything unsavory. He always maintained himself above reproach.

One of the reasons I was inspired to write about Dr. King was because he was my first pastor to depart into Glory. Out of all the pastors that I had, he was the first one to die.

I shall never forget the depth of the impact his departure had on me and the church. It was like the lights in the world went out and my eyes had to adjust to the darkness.

It has been said that when your Pastor dies, a part of you goes with him. I identify with that yet even as much, because the impartation of Dr. King in my life was so great, a part of him lives on in me. I am not alone. There are many spiritual daughters and sons who have been impacted by Dr. King. I am certain they will share their memories and testimonies on the appropriate social mediums that will be made available. It is my hope that those tributes and testimonials will enable us to produce a series of mini books about our beloved pastor. I am so exceedingly glad he passed this way.

The ABC's of Salvation

A. Admit that you have sinned. *"For all have sinned, and come short of the glory of God." (Romans 3:23)*

B. Believe on Jesus Christ the Savior. *"For God so loved the world, that he gave his only begotten Son, that whosoever Believeth in Him should not perish, but have everlasting life." (John 3:16)*

C. Confess. *"That if thou shalt confess with thy mouth the Lord Jesus and shalt believe in thine heart that God hath raised him from the dead, thou shalt be saved, For with the heart man believeth unto righteousness; and with the mouth confession is made unto salvation." (Romans 10: 9-10)*

A Prayer for Salvation

"Heavenly Father in Jesus name, I confess that I am a sinner. Forgive me for my sin and save me. I repent of my sin. I believe in my heart on the Lord Jesus Christ and confess with my mouth that I accept Him as my personal Lord and Saviour. Thank you for saving me. Amen."

BIOGRAPHICAL SKETCH OF THE AUTHOR

 Bishop Norman Lyons, Jr. is the founder and senior pastor of the Fountain of Life Church in Uniondale, New York. In addition to his national ministry, he has also done missionary work in Haiti, Nigeria, West Africa and Italy. Bishop Lyons has served as an executive council member of the International Council of Local Churches. He has also served as a member of M.E.C.C.A. For seven years Bishop Lyons was a Board Member of the New York Call hosted by Pastor Donnie McClurkin. Bishop Lyons is Chaplain Emeritus for the Long Island Conference of Clergy.

At the time of this writing, Bishop Lyons has been preaching for 42 years. He has been married to his darling wife, Pastor Sharon, for 41 years. They have pastored the Fountain of Life Church for 38 years.

Norman and Sharon are the grateful parents of two daughters, Juliet and Jasmine. They also have been blessed with a son-in-love, Joaquin, Juliet's husband.

www.ingramcontent.com/pod-product-compliance
Lightning Source LLC
Chambersburg PA
CBHW071203130626
46555CB00004B/1571